Animal Stories
for Little Children

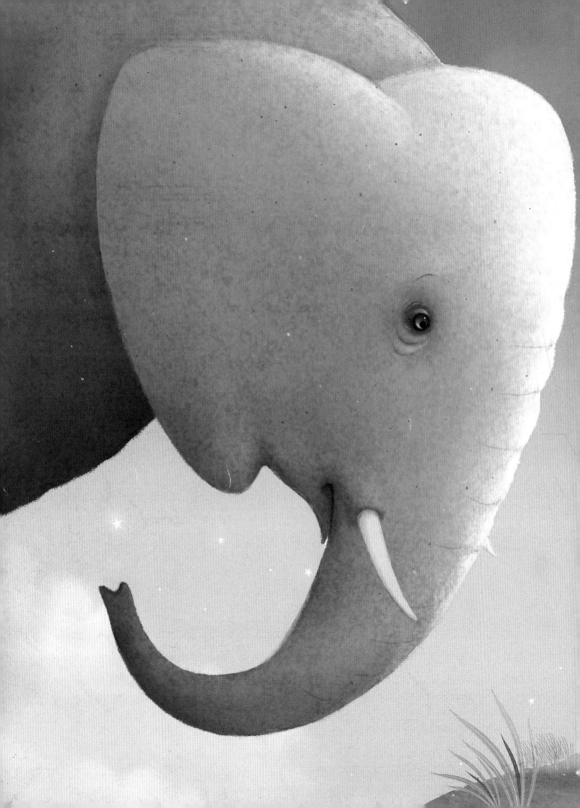

Animal Stories
for Little Children

Retold by Rosie Dickins
Illustrated by Richard Johnson

Contents

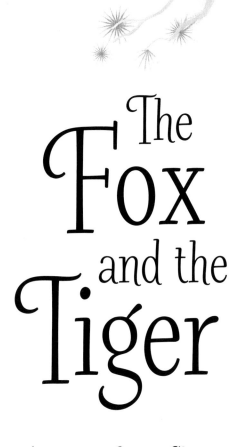

The Fox and the Tiger

A story from China

Deep in a forest of prickly pine trees,
there lived a **FIERCE TIGER**, with
dagger claws and deadly jaws.

The tiger liked to stretch
those jaws wide and...

ROARRRR!

...until the ground shook
and the trees trembled.

Uh-oh...

The little animals
shivered and quivered
and fled before the sound.

It's the tiger!
Run away.

"**EVERYONE** fears me,"
thought the tiger
proudly.

"I am the biggest.
I am the strongest.
I am the **FIERCEST** of all."

"I should be **RULER**
of this forest!"

The tiger stalked through the trees... and saw a squirrel nibbling a nut.

ROARR

RRR!

Eeeep

The squirrel squealed, dropped the nut
and scurried quickly away.

A little later, there was a rabbit,
enjoying a patch of juicy grass.

ROARRRR!

The rabbit jumped and disappeared
down a hole in a flash.

Meeep

The tiger chuckled and walked on,
prouder than ever.

"Everyone fears the
ruler of the forest!"

"I am the biggest.
I am the strongest.
I am the..."

"Wait... **WHAT?**"

A bushy-tailed fox was sitting
calmly on the path ahead.

The fox looked the tiger in
the eye and... smiled.

The tiger
opened
those jaws.

ROAR

The fox didn't flinch
or move an inch.

RRR!

The tiger scowled and growled.
"I am the ruler of the forest.
You should run in fear when
you hear my voice!"

"Ah, but I am the **RULER** of
RULERS," answered the fox.
"So you should be afraid of **ME!**"

"I've never heard of you,"
grumbled the tiger.

"The **OTHER** animals all
know me," shrugged the fox.

Come and
I'll show you.

They walked through the trees,
until they heard a bustling
and rustling in the undergrowth.
A little mouse was collecting berries.

The fox kept walking.

The mouse looked up, squealed –
and scampered away.

The tiger blinked in surprise.
"Still, it was only a mouse!"
the tiger muttered.

Squ-eeeeeeee-eak!

Next, they spied a grizzled wolf,
slinking through the trees ahead.

The fox kept walking.

The wolf glanced around...

Yow-ow-ow-owl

The tiger began to worry.
"The other animals DO fear this fox.
Perhaps I should too."

A little further on, a big, furry bear
was snoozing in a patch of sun.

Without a pause,
the fox walked up
and whispered...

Boo!

Startled, the bear awoke
to find TWO fierce faces
staring through the leaves.

Huh?

Quickly, the bear rose up
and stumbled away.

That was enough for the tiger,
who turned tail and fled.

I am sorry I doubted you,
oh Ruler of Rulers!

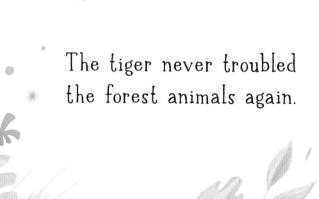

The tiger never troubled
the forest animals again.

The fox smiled and thought...

"Oh, Tiger, brute strength
is no match for brains!
It was **YOU** they were
afraid of, not me."

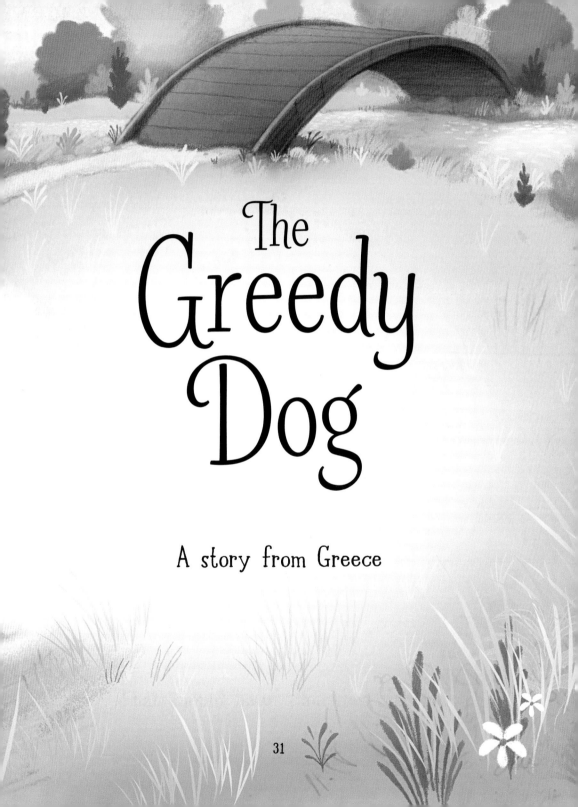

The Greedy Dog

A story from Greece

Dog dozed in the sun, dreaming of dinner...
mountains of **MEAT**, barrels of **BISCUITS**...
and a great big juicy **BONE**... **YUM!**

The dream was so real,
Dog could almost smell it.

No wait – I CAN smell something,

Dog thought, nose twitching.

Something BIG.
Something JUICY.

MMMMMMM...

Dog's mouth began to water.

That smells like a BONE!
Where is it?

Dog sniffed eagerly
in EVERY direction.

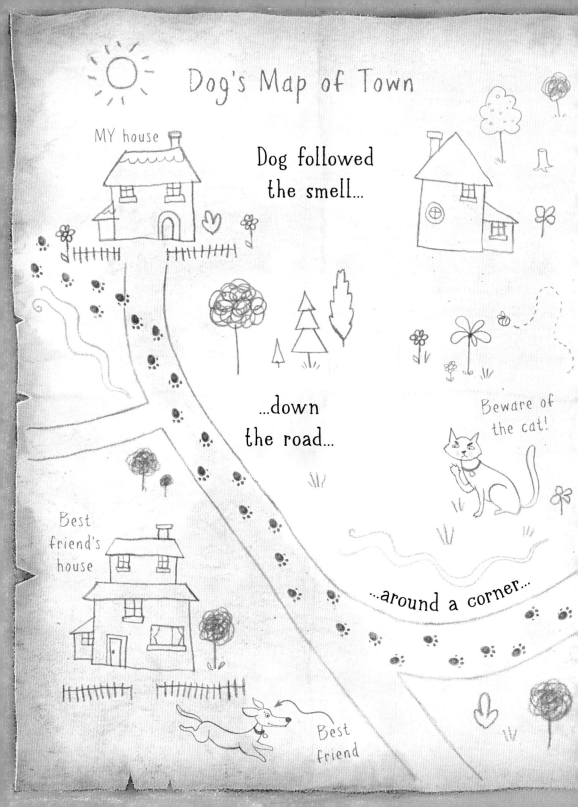

...to a butcher's shop.

Dog gazed through
the window
and drooled.

There, on the counter, was
a great big juicy bone!

I WANT IT!

The butcher was busy
serving a customer.

Dog looked left and right.
No one was watching.

Slowly, sneakily,
Dog crept inside and...

SNAP!

...clamped the bone between
strong, white teeth.

STOP!

cried the butcher.

But Dog didn't stop.
Dog **RAN**.

Now the road wound between grass and trees. Dog padded along proudly, very pleased with life.

A little way on, a stream burbled
below a low wooden bridge. Dog got
halfway across – then stopped.

What's THAT?

It looked like something in
the water. Dog trotted to the side
of the bridge and peered down.

There, below the bridge, was **ANOTHER** dog,
with **ANOTHER** great big juicy bone.

"Look at **THAT** bone," Dog thought.

It's even bigger and
juicier than mine.

Dog scowled at the other dog.
The other dog scowled back.

Dog gave a low, rumbling growl.
The other dog growled back.

Dog let out a fierce bark.

The other dog did
exactly the same.

GRRRRR... WOOF!

GRRRRR... WOOF!

The moment Dog's jaws opened,
the beautiful big bone tumbled out...

SPLOSH!

At the same moment, the
other dog disappeared –
along with **BOTH** bones.

NOOOOOOOOO!

Too late, Dog realized...
There WAS no other dog.
There was no other bone.
Only Dog's own reflection!

"Silly me," thought Dog, nodding
sheepishly at the reflection.

If only I hadn't been so greedy!

And the reflection nodded
back, as if to agree.

Why the Zebra has Stripes

A story from southern Africa

Long ago, when the world
was new, Zebra looked
very different.

Zebra had a smooth white
coat, a stiff white mane
and a tufty white tail –
without a single stripe.

In those early days, the sun blazed
down and it rarely rained.

The air was hot.
The ground was dry.

Zebra longed for a cool,
refreshing drink.

I'm SOOOO thirsty.

Luckily, Zebra knew where
to find a watering hole
brimming with cool, clear water.

Unluckily, a selfish baboon
had found it too.

Baboon wanted **ALL** the water
in the watering hole.

61

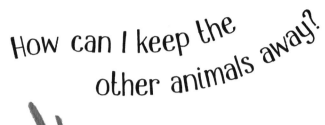

How can I keep the
other animals away?

Baboon glanced
around, then began
to gather armfuls
of dry sticks.

Baboon piled the sticks
into a straggly heap and
set fire to them.

Orange flames hissed
and crackled
and spat.

"That should help." chuckled Baboon.

The fire was burning brightly
when Zebra arrived.

As Zebra came closer, Baboon
jumped up and down
and **SCREAMED.**

Go away!
This water is MINE!

WHY?
asked Zebra
curiously.

Because I was here first!

snapped Baboon.

Now go away
or you'll regret it.

Zebra wasn't frightened.

"Behave yourself, you old Baboon."

This water is for EVERYONE.

NO! screeched Baboon.
"I won't let anyone drink it!"

We'll see about that,
whinnied Zebra,
pawing the ground.

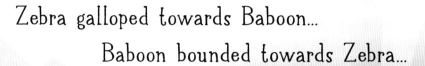

Zebra galloped towards Baboon...
Baboon bounded towards Zebra...

BAM!

OOF!

OW!

They collided in a confusion
of fur and hooves.

Baboon flew
into the air...

AAAAAAAAAAAAAAAAAA

AAAAAAAAAARGHHH

...and landed **SMACK**

in the middle of the fire.

Baboon jumped
up fast.

oooowww!

Oh no! Baboon's bottom was bright red and stung like anything.

Baboon still has a red bottom to this day.

The sticks from the fire
flew into the air.

They clattered down
on Zebra, leaving sooty
stripes all over.

Zebra still has stripes
to this day, and is quite
proud of the pattern.

And ALL the animals drink
from the watering hole
whenever they want.

Chicken Licken

A story from Europe

One bright, breezy day,
little Chicken Licken went for a walk.

WHOOOO-HOOOO-OOOOSH

The wind blew hard, sending
clouds rushing and leaves rustling.

BOP!

Something small and hard
bounced on Chicken Licken's head.

What was THAT?

Chicken Licken looked up and
saw the wide blue sky.

"It must have been
a piece of sky."

Oh no... the sky is falling in!

"I'd better run and
warn everyone."

Feathers aflutter, Chicken Licken
rushed off towards the farmyard.

There was Henny Penny,
looking about for worms.

Henny Penny, Henny Penny,
the sky is falling in!

"Oh no, what shall we do?"
squawked Henny Penny.

"I'm going to warn everyone!"
said Chicken Licken.

"I'll come too," Henny Penny
clucked and bustled
along behind.

Ducky Lucky was
splashing in the pond.

*Ducky Lucky, Ducky Lucky,
the sky is falling in!*

chirped Chicken Licken.

"Oh no, what shall we do?"
quacked Ducky Lucky.

"We're going to warn everyone!"
clucked Henny Penny.

"I'll come too," Ducky Lucky
decided and waddled
along behind.

Over the hill,
who did they see
but Goosey Loosey.

Goosey Loosey, Goosey Loosey, the sky is falling in!

chirped Chicken Licken.

"Oh no, what shall we do?"
honked Goosey Loosey.

"We are going to warn everyone!"
quacked Ducky Lucky.

"I'll come too," Goosey Loosey
announced and strutted
along behind.

Now Chicken Licken, Henny Penny,
Ducky Lucky and Goosey Loosey
hurried along together.

On the edge of the farmyard,
they met a fox with a bushy tail
and a broad grin. It was Foxy Loxy.

"What's the hurry, my fine feathered friends?" Foxy Loxy asked, in a voice dripping with honey.

"Oh Foxy Loxy," chirped Chicken Licken. "The sky is falling in! We're going to warn everyone."

Foxy Loxy nodded thoughtfully.

You must tell the farmer.
Follow me!

Foxy Loxy trotted over to an
old oak tree. There was a hole
in one side of the trunk.

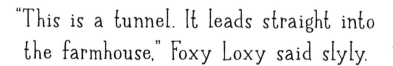

"This is a tunnel. It leads straight into
the farmhouse," Foxy Loxy said slyly.

"It's awfully dark," clucked Henny Penny
nervously. "I don't like the dark!"

"Don't be afraid of the **DARK**," said Foxy Loxy, grinning. "The **DARK** won't hurt you."

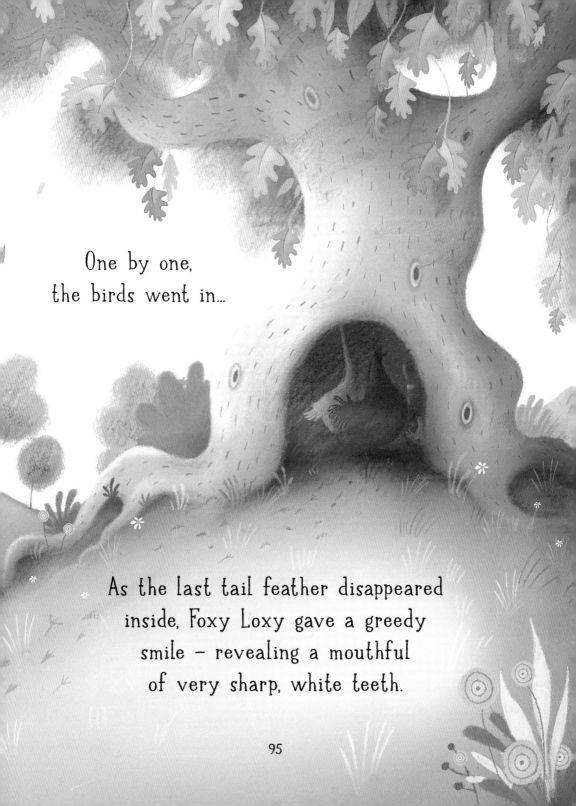

One by one,
the birds went in...

As the last tail feather disappeared
inside, Foxy Loxy gave a greedy
smile – revealing a mouthful
of very sharp, white teeth.

Time for dinner!

"We can't stop for dinner
while the sky is falling,"
said Chicken Licken.

"The sky ISN'T falling,
birdbrain," growled Foxy Loxy.
"And it's not time for YOUR
dinner. I meant MY dinner...

and I'm going to eat

YOU!"

Too late, the birds realized the
hole wasn't a shortcut... it was
a TRAP! And the only way out
was past Foxy Loxy.

Just then, the wind blew up again.

WHOOOO-HOOOO-OOOOSH!

The oak tree creaked.
Something small and hard bounced...

BOP!

...on Foxy Loxy's head.

Ow! What was that?

"The sky!" squawked
Chicken Licken.
"It really IS falling..."

Foxy Loxy looked
up nervously.

Another gust
shook the tree.

It was too much for Foxy Loxy.
That greedy fox turned tail and ran...

...never to be seen
in the farmyard again.

Henny Penny, Ducky Lucky and
Goosey Loosey burst out laughing.

That's not sky, those are ACORNS!

"Oh," said Chicken Licken, blushing.
"I didn't see them... sorry.
So the sky ISN'T falling then."

The other birds shook their heads.
"No, but don't tell Foxy Loxy!"

The Brave Little Hare

A story from India

It was a hot, cloudless summer.

Out on the plains, where the
elephants lived, the rivers and
waterholes were turning to mud.

But deep in the forest,
where the hares lived,
there was still one lake
of cool, blue water.

By day, the hares grazed on
the soft, sweet grass that
grew around the lake.

By night, they slept on the lakeshore,
while the moon shone over the water.

It was a calm, peaceful place.

At least, it WAS... until a herd
of thirsty elephants arrived.

A-ROOO-OOO!

They trumpeted loudly as
they trampled a path to
the water's edge.

Hares ran for cover
in all directions.

The elephants didn't notice.
They were too busy guzzling and
gulping and galumphing around.

The hares hid their heads
in their paws and hoped the
elephants would go away.

But they
didn't.

LONG trunks slurped
and sprayed.

HUGE feet stomped
and swayed.

Before long, the grass was flattened
and the ground was churned to mud.

"The elephants are destroying our home!" quivered an old hare.

What shall we do?

The other hares shook their heads. None of them had an answer.

Then a little hare piped up.

I have an idea!
Leave this to me.

The little hare waited for
nightfall, then hopped off to find
the leader of the elephants.

Excuse me?

The elephant didn't move.

Hello??

Still nothing.

HEY
YOU!

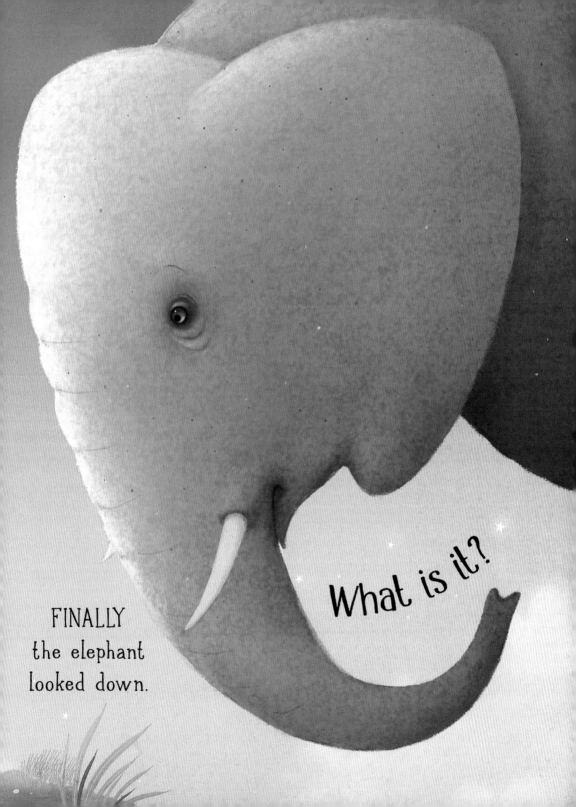

FINALLY
the elephant
looked down.

What is it?

"Oh enormous elephant,"
began the little hare. "This lake
belongs to Mighty Moon.
You elephants are disturbing
Mighty Moon's rest."

WHAT Mighty Moon?
snorted the elephant.

You haven't heard
of Mighty Moon?

"No," said the elephant.

"Mighty Moon is the **RULER** of the night sky," said the hare.

"A **VERY** powerful person, who **HATES** to be disturbed!"

The elephant began to feel worried.

"Mighty Moon comes to sleep in this lake each night," the hare went on. "Look!"

The little hare stretched out a paw and pointed.

Large and round and silvery,
the face of the moon glowed
mysteriously on the dark water.

Curious, the elephant
reached out...

As soon as the tip of the elephant's trunk touched the surface, the moon began to

shiver and shake.

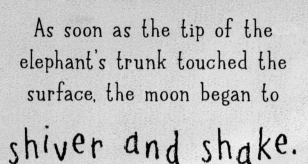

Oh NO,
exclaimed the hare.
"Mighty Moon is
shaking with anger!"

The elephant backed away hastily.

"Apologies, Mighty Moon.
We'll leave here right away,
I promise."

To the elephant's relief,
the moon slowly
stopped shaking.

The leader of the elephants
hurried to rouse the herd.

"We must leave AT ONCE.
Before Mighty Moon
gets angry again!"

Moments later, the
elephants went.

As the last elephant tail
vanished between the trees,
a cheer went up from the hares.

"You did it," they told the
brave little hare. "Thank you!"

Now the lake was calm and peaceful
once more. The hares sighed happily
and snuggled down to sleep.

About the stories

The stories in this book are based on
traditional tales from around the world.

The Fox and the Tiger – this Chinese story is over
two thousand years old. It inspired the modern
story "The Gruffalo" and a Chinese saying:
"The fox assumes the might of the tiger."

The Greedy Dog – this is from Aesop's Fables,
a collection of stories designed to teach a
"moral" or lesson. They were written over
two thousand years ago in Ancient Greece.

Why the Zebra has Stripes – a very old story
told across southern Africa, this is one of many
traditional tales which explain how things came to be.

Chicken Licken (also known as "Chicken Little") –
told across Europe, this story was first
written down about two hundred years ago,
although the story itself is older.

The Brave Little Hare (also known as "Moon Lake") –
this comes from a collection of animal stories
written for three young Indian princes,
over two thousand years ago.

Designed by Samantha Barrett,
Tabitha Blore and Lenka Hrehova
Digital imaging: Nick Wakeford
Series designer: Russell Punter
Series editor: Lesley Sims